BAD BITCH
BLAM
BLAM
BLAM
AF421921

FLY?
DAY OF THE HORSEMEN
G-GOT THE KEYS.
HOW DO YOU AND FLY KNOW EACH OTHER?
SULTRA WAS MY RIDE OR DIE BITCH WHEN I WAS IN THE STREETS HEAVY.
S-SULTRA?
OH SHIT FLY! YOU AIGHT? YOU BANGED YO HEAD PRETTY HARD THERE.
YEAH, I'M GOOD, I'M GOOD! YOU KNOW YOU A STRAIGHT SAVAGE. ALWAYS MY DAY ONE, SHORTY. YOU STILL LOOKING TREACHEROUS.

YOU'VE ALWAYS BEEN A G.
I HAVE TO STAND ON BUSINESS FLY. I SEE THE SKATEBOARD MORPHADINES PULLED UP ON YOU AND YOUR CREW.
MORPHADINES?
YEAH, WHATCHU MESSIN' WITH THEM FOR? FIRE MAKES THEM TRANSFORM TO SOME NASTY CREATURES.
I, UH....
THESE TWO LAMES WITH YOU?
YEAH. SULTRA, THIS IS MY HOMIE CLIPSE, AND MY MANAGER FRANK.
WHAT THE FUCK JUST HAPPENED?
YA'LL JUST ENCOUNTERED A CLASS C MORPHADINE. IT'S LEVELS TO THEM NASTY BASTARDS.
MORPH-TRACK
I'VE BEEN TRACKING A PACK OF THEM WITH MY NEW APP.

AND HOW LONG HAVE YOU BEEN HUNTING THESE MORPHADINES?

OH, FEW YEARS. EVER SINCE THEY ATTACKED ONE OF MY GIRLS. TORE HER ENTIRE FUCKIN FACE OFF.

THEY DIDN'T EVEN HAVE THE DECENCY TO COVER HER HEAD UP THEY JUST LEFT HER OUT THERE LIKE ROADKILL.

HEARTLESS BASTARDS.

THIS IS CRAZY BECAUSE JUST LIKE, THE WEIRDEST SHIT HAS BEEN HAPPENING TODAY, AND THE WORLD JUST SEEMS OK WITH IT.

WHAT DO YOU MEAN?

MY LABEL CEO TURNED INTO A FUCKIN VAMPIRE EARLIER.

A VAMPIRE? NEVER SEEN ONE, BUT I'VE HEARD STORIES. MAYBE THE MORPHADINES ARE A HYBRID OF THEM. I AIN'T NEVER WORRIED BOUT YOU FLY. YOU THAT NIGGA.

I NEED A STIFFER FUCKIN' DRINK. SOUNDS LIKE SOME SHIT OUT OF A BAD HORROR MOVIE. JESUS.

IT'S REAL SHIT IN THESE STREETS. OUT OF THIS WORLD SHIT. WHAT Y'ALL GETTIN' INTO?
WE FINNA HEAD DOWNTOWN TO CHECK OUT THE ABANDONED SUBWAY. WE GOTTA HANDLE SOME SHIT.
YOU WANT A TOUR DOWN THERE? I HEARD IT'S WEIRD AS FUCK DOWN THERE.
YOU AIN'T BEEN DOWN THERE?
NAH, NOT ME. BUT MY WEED GUY WITH THE "DRAGON-KUSH", VIRGIL. HE USED TO RUN THESE 'HIGH & HAUNTED' SMOKING WALKING TOURS DOWN THERE, UNTIL THEY SEALED IT UP. BUT IF ANYONE STILL KNOWS A WAY IN, IT'D BE HIM.
THAT'S WHAT'S UP, THANKS BAE. I HOPE THIS NIGGA'S OFFICIAL.
I'LL SHOOT HIM A TEXT THEN HIT YOU UP WITH A MEETING SPOT. HE'S LOW-KEY LIKE THAT. HE'S SOLID AS THEY COME, FLY.
DOPE. YOU STILL GOT MY CELL NUMBER?
NOW HOW COULD I EVER DELETE MY FLYBOY?
NOW FLY AWAY, MY BLACK DOVE.
BAD BITCH

WE GOTTA GET TO THIS FUCKIN' SUBWAY.
FUUUUUCK. DID YOU KNOW THAT OLD SUBWAY IS OVER TEN MILES LONG? EVEN IF THIS DUDE KNOWS A WAY IN, HOW WE GON' FIND THE EXACT SPOT MY NIGGA REIGN STAR WAS HELD UP IN?
1638
DOPEFLY
MAYBE WE COULD GET A BLOODHOUND.
WHAT IS WITH YOU AND THESE FUCKIN' BLOODHOUNDS? YOU THE HOMIE CLIPSE, BUT YOU CAN BE A WEIRD MUHFUCKA SOMETIMES.
I JUST THINK THEY'RE THE WOLVERINES OF THE CANINE WORLD.
THE... FUCK?
VRROOOOM
SMASH

CHK
CHK

YO! WHO THE FUCK ARE THESE NIGGAS IN THAT CAR.. THEY LOOK CRAZY THAN A MUTHAFUCKA!
SHIT! YO THEY SHOOTIN AT US BRO, YOU GOT A HAMMER OR A CHOPPER IN THIS BITCH?
THUNK
PULL OVER. I GOTTA GET THEIR INSURANCE INFO. WORSE DAY EVER.
STRAP UP MY DUDES. IT'S HEREDITARY MAFIA CHASING US! WE GOTTA GET THE FUCK OUTTA HERE BIG HOMIE!
BLAMMM BLAMMM
POP POP POP POP POP POP
SPLLIK
SHWUNK

THWWII
I SURE FUCKIN DO, 2 NINES UNDER YOUR SEAT! I'M 10 TOES DOWN, FLY!
BLAM BLAM
POPP POPP POPP
SHIT! DEAD END!
SCREEEEEEEEEECHHHHH
BAIL!
FUCK! I'M OUT OF BULLETS!

COMPLACENCY KILLS. OUR CAUSE MUST LOOK FORWARD, TO THE FUTURE.
HERE!
FLY, FULL DISCLOSURE. I'VE BEEN RUNNING FROM ONE HABIT TO ANOTHER, HIDING BEHIND THESE... PILLS. JOEY GAVE PUSHED THEM ON ME, SAID THEY'D KEEP ME 'SAFE', PREVENT ME FROM BECOMING...ONE OF THEM.
YOU KNEW? ABOUT THE VAMPIRES? ARE YOU ONE OF THESE FUCKERS?
MORE LIKE, I WAS TOO SCARED TO ADMIT IT. NO, I'M A HYBRID BEING MADE UP OF EVERYTHING. BUT NO MORE. AYE, WE GOTTA SPLIT UP! NOW!
HEY, AIN'T THAT THAT FAMOUS RAPPER, FLYBOY OR SUMTIN'?
WHAT THE FUCK IS EVERYTHING, MY DUDE?
TAKE BACK OUR COUNTRY!
WOLFE 4 PREZ
NO WOKE!
I'M NO. 2 GREEN ENERGY!
WOLFE
HEY, THAT'S HIM!
BACK TO 1950
ANTI WOKE
NO C
FUCK GREEN ENERGY
WOLFE FOR PRESID
FOREIGN PIRATES, PEDOPHILES, AND PREDATORS USE THE INTERNET TO MANIPULATE THEIR FACES. TOYING WITH OUR SENSE OF SECURITY. PAVING AN IMMORAL WASTELAND FOR FUTURE GENERATIONS TO WANDER AIMLESSLY.
FOR TOO LONG WE'VE DEALT WITH LOOSE WEB REGULATIONS, AND EVEN LOOSER POLITICIANS. I SAY, CUT 'EM LOOSE..
GET HIM OUT OF THERE.
THAT'S A FAMOUS RAPPER. HE COULD BE THE KEY TO GETTING THE BLACK VOTE.

MY NAME IS JAMES WOLFE, AND AS YOUR NEXT PRESIDENT, I PLAN ON BUILDING A NEW NON WOKE WORLD! WEB 4 IS OURS!!
ANTI WOKE WORLD!
ANTI WOKE WORLD!
ANTI WOKE WORLD!
AND THE LIBS ARE GONNA PAY FOR IT!
YO, OVER HERE!
THE HELL, DUDE?
COME WITH ME.
IT'S NOT ME YOU HAVE TO WORRY ABOUT!
DUDE ARE YOU A FUCKIN' WHOLE ZOMBIE OR SOMETHING?
I'M YOUR FUCKIN' WORST NIGHTMARE!
FUCK. WOLFE'S FEDS GOT HIM.
LET'S GET OUTTA HERE.
WE'LL TALK ABOUT THAT CRAZY SHIT LATER!
YO, FLY!
FLY, AYE, FLY!

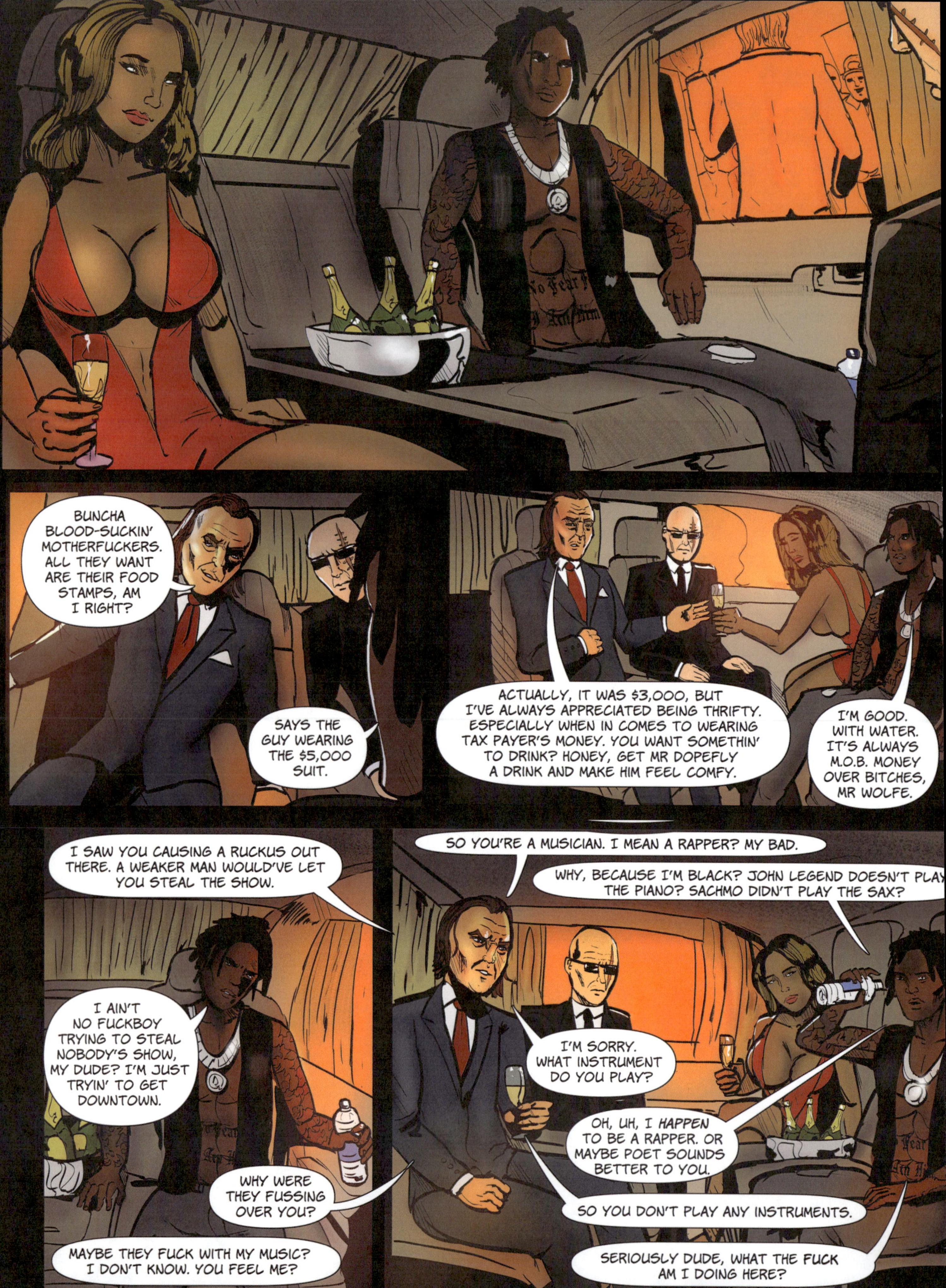

BUNCHA BLOOD-SUCKIN' MOTHERFUCKERS. ALL THEY WANT ARE THEIR FOOD STAMPS, AM I RIGHT?
SAYS THE GUY WEARING THE $5,000 SUIT.
ACTUALLY, IT WAS $3,000, BUT I'VE ALWAYS APPRECIATED BEING THRIFTY. ESPECIALLY WHEN IN COMES TO WEARING TAX PAYER'S MONEY. YOU WANT SOMETHIN' TO DRINK? HONEY, GET MR DOPEFLY A DRINK AND MAKE HIM FEEL COMFY.
I'M GOOD. WITH WATER. IT'S ALWAYS M.O.B. MONEY OVER BITCHES, MR WOLFE.
I SAW YOU CAUSING A RUCKUS OUT THERE. A WEAKER MAN WOULD'VE LET YOU STEAL THE SHOW.
I AIN'T NO FUCKBOY TRYING TO STEAL NOBODY'S SHOW, MY DUDE? I'M JUST TRYIN' TO GET DOWNTOWN.
WHY WERE THEY FUSSING OVER YOU?
MAYBE THEY FUCK WITH MY MUSIC? I DON'T KNOW. YOU FEEL ME?
SO YOU'RE A MUSICIAN. I MEAN A RAPPER? MY BAD.
WHY, BECAUSE I'M BLACK? JOHN LEGEND DOESN'T PLAY THE PIANO? SACHMO DIDN'T PLAY THE SAX?
I'M SORRY. WHAT INSTRUMENT DO YOU PLAY?
OH, UH, I HAPPEN TO BE A RAPPER. OR MAYBE POET SOUNDS BETTER TO YOU.
SO YOU DON'T PLAY ANY INSTRUMENTS.
SERIOUSLY DUDE, WHAT THE FUCK AM I DOING HERE?

WELL I WAS LITTLE JEALOUS OF ALL THE ATTENTION YOU WERE GETTING. I WAS GONNA DRUG YA AND DUMP YA OUT IN THE MIDDLE OF THE WOODS.
YOU A BITCH AND I AIN'T VOTIN FOR YOU OR ANYBODY THAT FUCKS WITH YOU.
BUT NOW I'M THINKIN', MAYBE YOU CAN HELP ME OUT WITH MY LITTLE URBAN VOTE PROBLEM.
THE BROTHAS AND SISTAS JUST AIN'T VOTIN' RED NO MO'. WE NEED YO' PEOPLE TO FALL IN LINE. WE'LL GIVE YOU ANOTHER GOLD CHAIN AND A CAR. Y'ALL NOT SMART ENOUGH TO START HEDGE FUNDS TOGETHER AND BUILD GENERATIONAL WEALTH. YA'LL WILL JUST COMPETE AGAINST EACH AND FUCK IT UP ANYWAY.
WELL, I'M SORRY TO HEAR THAT. TRULY, I AM. I'M TRYING TO HELP YOUR NIGGRA NATION OUT MR FLY.
THE FUCK'D YOU..
YOU....
YOU DRUGGED ME, YOU LAME PIECE OF SH....

EH, WHAT THE DEVIL IS GOING ON HERE?
SHRIP
I DON'T KNOW. WHAT THE FUCK DUDE, YOU'RE BRITISH? DUDE, YOU LOOK LIKE MY NIGGA EMINEM.
WHAT? AHEM... NAH, MAN, FUCK THOSE PATTINGTON BEAR-LOOKIN' MOTHERFUCKERS.
THE BOOK OF FENRIR, CHAPTER 1, VERSE 6.
THE FUCK DO YOU WANT?
HERE WE ARE. AND BY THE GIANTESS ANGRBODA, LOKI BORE THREE CHILDREN: JORMUNGAND, THE SERPENT, HEL, THE DEATH-GODDESS, AND FENRIR, THE WOLF.
PLEASE, DON'T HURT ME.

BUT THE GODS HAD TERRIBLE FOREBODINGS CONCERNING THE DESTINY OF THESE THREE CHILDREN. IN ORDER TO KEEP THEM AT BAY, THEY THREW JOMUNGAND TO THE OCEAN AND HEL TO THE UNDERWORLD.
FENRIR, HOWEVER, INSPIRED TOO MUCH FEAR FOR THEM TO LET HIM OUT FROM UNDER THEIR WATCHFUL EYES. SO THE GODS REARED FENRIR IN ASGARD, AND FROM A PUP, HE QUICKLY GREW TO MONSTROUS PROPORTIONS.
KNOWING WELL HOW MUCH DEVASTATION HE WOULD CAUSE IF HE EVER WERE TO ESCAPE, THE GODS SAW NO CHOICE BUT TO BLIND THE WOLF WITH HOT IRONS, BIND HIM IN CHAINS FROM THE DWARF REALM, AND PRY HIS JAWS OPEN WITH A SWORD.

THERE, IN THIS SORDID STATE, FENRIR REMAINS.
IN HIS NAME.... WE HUNT.
HOLY SHIT.
AWOOOOOO
...FUCKIN' WITH ME.
THESE LAMES ARE WEREWOLVES?
GOTTA BE THE WEED...
SNIF

RUN.
SNIFFFF
THIS ISN'T WHAT I SIGNED UP FOR. MAKE SOME MONEY, THEY SAID. TRICK THE DUMB AMERICANS, THEY SAID.
SHIT. YOU AGAIN.
YOU THINK I DEVOTED MY CHILDHOOD TO THE THEATER TO BE KNOWN FOR HIPPY-HOPPY MUSIC.
ASHH

WHAT'S THE LAST THING YOU REMEMBER?
AFTERNOON TEA. I THOUGHT THE BLACK LEAVES HAD GONE BAD BUT, THEY MUST'VE DRUGGED ME. OH, STUPID, STUPID, MARSHALL.
LISTEN, MY NIGGA, I FUCKS WIT' YOU AND IF WE GOT EACH OTHERS BACK, I THINK WE CAN MAKE IT THROUGH THIS. I USED TO TAKE MY HOES CAMPING FOR TEAM BUILDING ALL THE TIME, SO I KNOW MY WAY AROUND THESE WOODS.
YOU DO WHAT YOU DO PLEASE. I'M STAYING RIGHT HER
THESE MUFUKAS WILL SNIFF YO ASS OUT MY DUDE, I PROMISE YOU THAT. WE GOTTA MOVE.
I'M OUTTA HERE, G!
AWOOOOOO

FUCK!!! HELP ME!!!!! AHHHHH!!!!
HOMIE IS FUCKED! DAMN.
SNAP
WHERE IS THE BLOOD MIC?
KRASH
SKRUNT

SWIPE
THRUD
STAB

FLYBOY, HOW YOU FEELIN' MAN?
HE'S WAKING UP.
YOU HAD US WORRIED THERE FOR A BIT, MY MAN.
I'D FEEL A WHOLE LOT BETTER IF YOU GET SOME OF THEM ONLYFANS BITCHES UP HERE, AND SOME CHAMPAGNE MY NIGGA.
EASY. YOU LOST A LOTTA BLOOD, SO YOU NEED A TRANSFUSION.
BLOOD?
YEAH, SO YOU'RE GONNA GET TIRED REAL QUICKLY, SO I NEED YOU TO REST.
THE WOLVES...
THE WHAT?
WHAT HAPPENED TO THE WEREWOLVES?
WEREWOLVES?
YOU ALSO SUSTAINED A MODERATE CONCUSSION. FIBULA FRACTURED IN THREE PLACES. SHATTERED WRIST.
WHAT HAPPENED?
I KNEW I SHOULDN'T HAVE LET HIM FUCKIN' DRIVE HOME AFTER HIS RELEASE PARTY AT MOON'S. THIS IS ALL MY FAULT. FUCK! I NEED TO FIND A BAR!
YOU HAD A CAR ACCIDENT, DUDE. HIT AND RUN ACTUALLY.

I REMEMBER DRIVING HOME.
THAT'S GOOD.
BUT THEN EVERYTHING GOT MAD CRAZY AFTER THAT. YOU TELLIN' ME NONE OF THAT WAS REAL?
BAD DREAMS FROM YOUR BRAIN SWELLING. I CAN ASSURE YOU, THERE ARE NO VAMPIRES OR WEREWOLVES HERE.
TO BE CONTINUED...

COMING SOON...

COMING SOON...

DOPÉFLY
Available at Dopefly.net
Take a deep dive into the
Dopefly Universe...
DOPE
DOPÉFLY
DOPÉFLY
DOPE